Practice Ma
Better

Written by Ruthie Godfrey

Illustrated by Helen Ayle

Ruthie Godfrey Books, LLC

ISBN: 978-1-952402-06-7 (Paperback)
ISBN: 978-1-952402-07-4 (Hardcover)
ISBN: 978-1-952402-08-1 (Ebook)
Library of Congress Control Number: 2020908762

For more information, email: ruthiegodfreybooks@gmail.com www.RuthieGodfreyBooks.com

Dedicated to Rebecca, who helped me to see myself as a writer.

And to my mom, who helped me to see myself as an author.

Stephen was a good athlete.

No, Stephen was a GREAT athlete.
When it came to running, he was the fastest. When it came to basketball, he could jump the highest. When it came to baseball, he could hit the farthest. When it came to soccer, he could dribble past anyone. He liked sports. No, he LOVED sports. Stephen felt like he was amazing at sports, so he spent all of his time playing and thinking about playing sports.

Stephen was a *great* athlete.

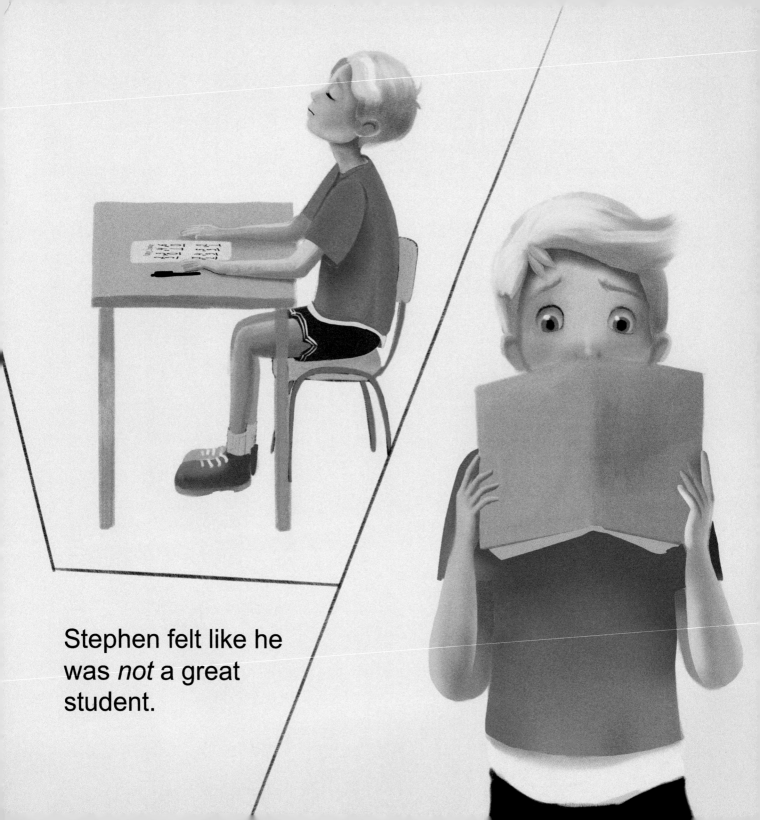

Stephen felt like he was *not* a great student.

When it came to reading, it seemed like he was the slowest. When it came to writing, he struggled to get a sentence on the page. When it came to multiplication tests, he got stuck on his 3's. He disliked school. No, he DESPISED school. He felt like he was horrible at school, so he spent as little time as possible thinking about school.

Stephen felt like he was a *terrible* student.

It was Wednesday. Again. Wednesday was Stephen's *least* favorite day of the week, the day of the timed multiplication test. It felt like every week was the same thing. Pencil ready, turn over paper, brain freeze, test blank.

"Stephen, I already started the timer. Are you okay?"
Mrs. Redmond's voice pulled Stephen out of his daze.

"Oh, I didn't hear you..." The truth was that Stephen
had given up before he'd even begun.

Mrs. Redmond gave Stephen a little pat on the shoulder and continued circling around the classroom.
Stephen could hear the scratching of frantic pencils on paper all around him. But he just stared at his blank paper. He picked up his pencil, but the right answers refused to come to his brain.

Beepbeepbeep, beepbeepbeep, beepbeepbeep.

"Everyone, hold your papers up!" When Mrs. Redmond finished collecting everyone's tests, she announced, "Time for lunch!"

Stephen scrambled out of his chair, shoved it halfway under his desk, and raced for the door.

"Stephen! Could you come back for just a moment, please?" Mrs. Redmond's voice caught Stephen in the doorway.

"*I was so close to recess!*" he thought. But he obediently dragged himself back from his favorite part of the day and into the classroom.

"Yes, Mrs. Redmond?"

"I couldn't help but notice your test, Stephen."

Stephen slowly made his way to Mrs. Redmond's desk. He could see his name at the top of the test that she was holding up.

"Your test is blank. I'm wondering, what happened?"

"Actually, it's not completely blank." Stephen pointed to the smiley faces that he'd drawn in all of the zeros on the entire test.

Mrs. Redmond raised an eyebrow. Stephen shrugged his shoulders and stared down at his shoes. He could not bring himself to look directly into her eyes.

"I'm just bad at school." Stephen shrugged again.

"Can I ask, how much did you practice this week?"

"Ummmm…… not that much." Stephen couldn't bear to tell her the truth, which was "*not at all*."

"Listen, Stephen. It shows when you practice. And it shows when you *don't* practice. When I was growing up, my teachers would always say 'Practice makes perfect!' but I don't believe that's true. Even when you practice, you might not get it perfect. But you know what you *will* get?"

Stephen forced himself to look up

"You'll get better, Stephen! Think about those multiplication facts as if you're shooting baskets. I bet you missed quite a few baskets when you first started. Everyone misses at first. You still miss sometimes, but the more you practice, the fewer times you miss!"

It was true, Stephen was really good at shooting baskets now. But he could also remember when he first started and wasn't so good at it. His older brother coached him on where to stand, how to hold the ball, and how to flick his wrist just right to get that perfect *swoosh*.

Stephen was a great athlete now… Could he maybe be a good student, too?

"You can do it, Stephen." This time Stephen looked his teacher right in the eye.

"Alright, I'll *try* to practice this week." Stephen didn't want to get his teacher's hopes up too high.

Really, he didn't want to get his *own* hopes up too high.

The rest of the day was a blur. Stephen was busy visualizing himself practicing and passing his next multiplication test. It was a strategy he learned from his basketball coach, to *visualize success*. It never occurred to him that he could use it with his school work, too. He could hardly wait to get home and make flashcards for practicing.

Stephen made up his mind.
*"I will not give up before I
give it another try."*

Throughout the entire week, Stephen flipped through his flashcards at breakfast, lunch, and dinner, walking home from school, sitting in the car, during commercial breaks on TV, and right before bed.

It wasn't easy. It was actually *really* hard work. At first. But the more that Stephen did it, the easier it got.

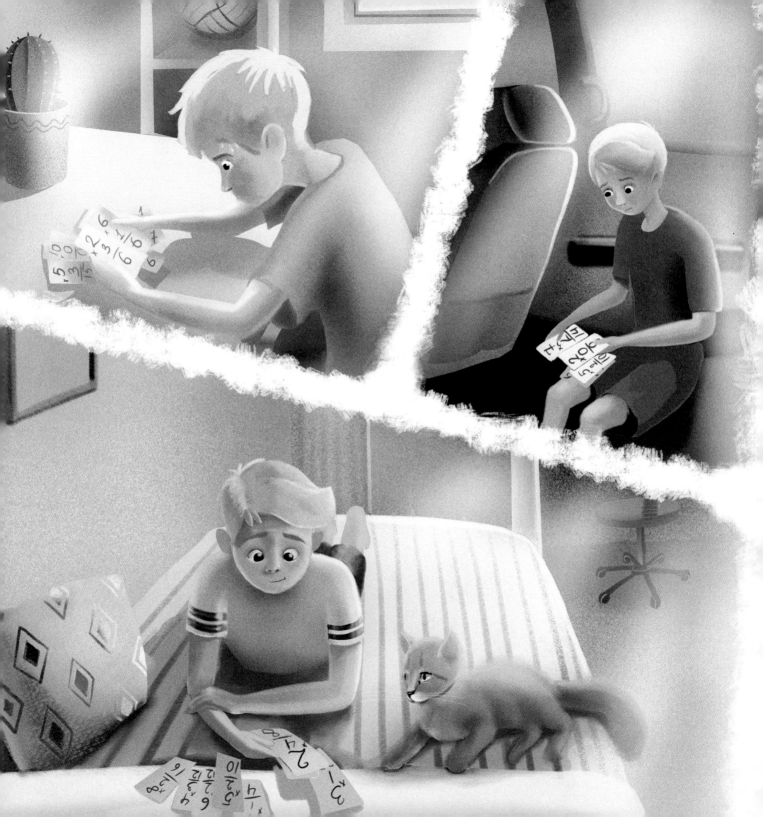

And just like that, it was Wednesday again. The day of the timed multiplication test. Every week *used to* be the same. Pencil ready, turn over paper, brain freeze, blank test.

This week felt different though.

Stephen felt like his brain was a little bit stronger.

Actually, his brain felt **a lot** stronger.

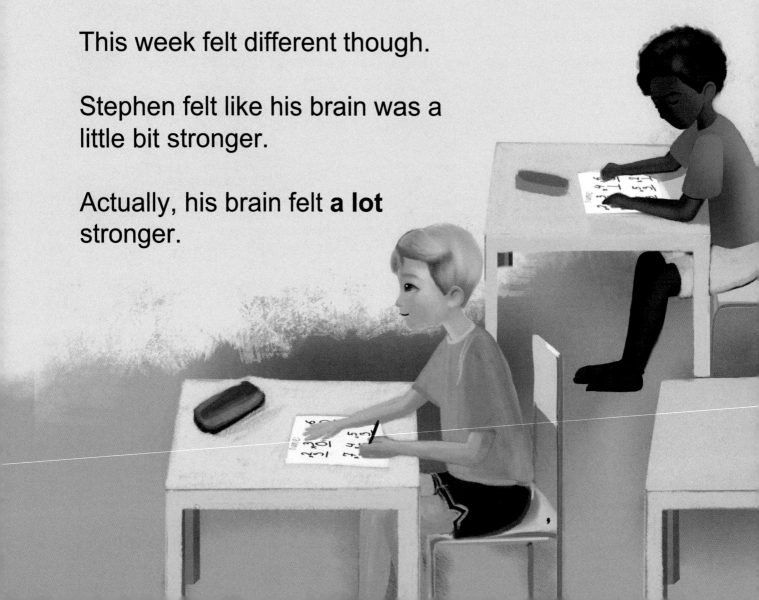

"Ready... set... GO!"

Stephen whipped his paper over. His pencil danced across the page as he confidently jotted down all of the answers to the test.

As soon as he scrawled the last answer, his hand shot up, victoriously waving his completed paper just as he heard the familiar *beepbeepbeep, beepbeepbeep, beepbeepbeep*.

Mrs. Redmond grinned at Stephen as she reached for his paper.

"Wow, Stephen, I can see you must have practiced!"

"I sure did! And practice does make *better*!!"

Stephen felt really proud of himself.

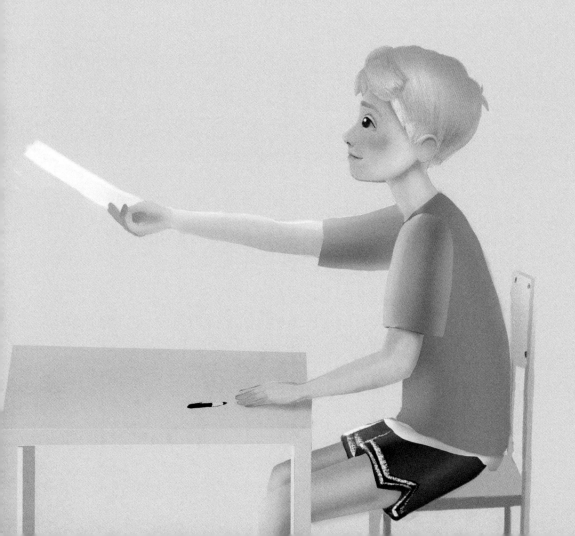

Where our adventure begins

Stephen knew he was a great athlete.

And, now, he believed he could be a great student, too. It would just take some practice to keep getting *better*.

About the Author

Ruthie Godfrey is an elementary teacher and author, dedicated to sharing important themes and truths about life. When she is not busy in the classroom, she writes children's books to both entertain and teach kids. She bases many of her stories on her observations of her students and their struggles in life. She is grateful for the opportunity to share virtues and love through stories, like a ray of light in a world that can feel a little bit dark at times.

Follow Ruthie at RuthieGodfreyBooks.com to subscribe to her newsletter for updates and promotions!

Author, Ruthie Godfrey

About the Illustrator

Helen Ayle was born in Kazakhstan, where her surname in Kazakhstan's language means "took pity and gave," She loves the meaning of her name. Helen is also an artist. She loves drawing and playing piano, kittens and chocolate (but who doesn't love chocolate?!) As an artist, she can tell you for certain that practice DOES make better! The first drawings she ever made when she was five years old were not great, in her opinion. Her mom told her they were pretty, though. She went on to spend eight years studying art in art school and college. And she can see a big improvement between her first drawings and the drawings she makes now. She still continues to study and improve in her artwork. When you practice, you can see improvement, too. Yes, sometimes it is hard. Yes, sometimes you don't see progress right away. But success will show up if you don't give up!

Illustrator, Helen Ayle

Dear Families and Teachers of all kinds,

As an elementary school teacher, I love to use stories as launching-points for conversations. I often watch my students struggle with their own beliefs in themselves. I especially feel for the students who struggle with academics. I always want to encourage them to understand that they are not alone in their struggle to do well in school. I want them to realize they can put the work in and see results. We often talk about the "growth mindset," which is based on the understanding that we maybe can't do it *yet*. "Yet" is a little word that has a lot of power! Our brains are growing and changing every day, and we can make great progress when we put forth consistent effort. I hope that you can encourage your own children to keep practicing, to keep building those connections in their brains, and to keep at the hard work, because it is worth it!

Colossians 3:23 - "Work willingly at whatever you do, as though you were working for the Lord rather than for people."

Check out some other books by Ruthie Godfrey!

And follow her author page for updates!

And please consider leaving us a REVIEW!!

Made in the USA
Middletown, DE
22 August 2020